The Story of
ZACHARY ZWEEN

By Mabel Watts ⚘ Illustrated by Marylin Hafner

PARENTS' MAGAZINE PRESS · NEW YORK

Other Books by Mabel Watts
The Narrow Escapes of Solomon Smart
The Boy Who Listened to Everyone
Henrietta and the Hat
Something for You, Something for Me
Weeks and Weeks
The Bed of Thistledown
A Little from Here, a Little for There

*To Bill, who followed me
all around London while
I followed Zachary Zween.*

Albert Ames went first each day,
Because his name began with A.
For A to Z, that was the rule

Of this particular London school.
"A to Z, boys," said Miss Midge,
When walking over London Bridge.

As Albert headed up the line
He said, "First place is ALWAYS mine!
I'm first on walking tours, and games,
Because I have the best of names!"

And who came last?
Poor Zachary Zween—
So envious that his face turned green!
Yes, Zachary Zween got most upset
And angry at the alphabet.

In class, t'was A to Z for spelling,
For history and storytelling.
For recess and arithmetic,
For jumping in the gym,
T'was Albert first,
And Zachary last.
No one came after HIM!

With lessons over for the day,
The teacher often led the way
Across a meadow (called a mead).
Behind her came the boys, with speed.

And Albert Ames was in the lead.
But who came last?
Why, Zachary.... See?
Because his name began with Z.

Out to Hyde Park, last in line,
Zack sailed his boat on the Serpentine.

Last in line to Marble Arch,
And famed Trafalgar Square—

Last to sit upon the lions
That guard the statue there.

But Albert Ames went first each day,
Because his name began with A.
When to the Queen Al carried roses,
He had the most upturned of noses.

And he was first to feed the swans
That float along the river—
First to wander through the Tower,
And give a little shiver—

First in line to see the Palace—
And the place where the March Hare
First met Alice.
First to see the changing guard . . .

And first indoors, while hailstones hard
Poured down on Zack,
Out in the yard!
"To make a fuss," Zack thought, "is silly.

"Who wants to be a Whining Willie?
Since Zachary Zween is my real name,
And always will remain the same,
Why not make *going last* a game?"

Being last meant LAST,
And yet,
A boy could find a horse
To pet
Along the way ...
And then,
Catch up to pick
Miss Midge a buttercup—
Or help a
Helpless little cat—
And other
Useful things like that.

Being last, Zack saw just how
The sidewalk artist draws a cow—
A speckled fish—
Grapes in a dish—
Or anything that you might wish.

Being last, you run or trot
On gravel path or grassy plot.
You find out what is wet—
And likewise, what is not!

One day they walked too far afield,
(Almost halfway to the Weald!)
The boys were tired, and it was late.

Miss Midge was in a dreadful state.
"We can't return on foot," she said.
"We'll have to take this train instead!"

Each boy found a seat inside
Where he could rest his feet and ride.

The train stood puffing on the track.
There was room for everyone... BUT ZACK!

Each coach was filled, from door to door—
And no more trains till half-past four!
Poor Zachary was filled with gloom.

"Ride
with me
Son..."

Each coach was packed. There was no room—
Until the guard, a friendly man,
Said, "Ride with me, son, in my van!

"Come follow me, and be my guest."
"I'm so excited!" Zack confessed.
Albert Ames rode way up front,

As cross as he could be.
Zack rode in back, for luckily,
HIS name began with Z.

He rode the guard's van, at the end,
And as the train went round the bend,
He helped the guard apply his brake—

He shared his crumpets and his cake.
What a ride!
Oh, what a lark!
When they got home it was quite dark.

"BEING LAST, I'D LIKE TO BE!"
Said Albert Ames, quite sulkily.
"For after all is said and done,
You look as if you'd had great fun!"

"I did indeed," said Zachary Zween.
"And nevermore will I turn green
Because I can't go *first*,
Like YOU,
To Hampstead Heath,
And the London Zoo.

"Will I be envious?
Not at all,
When we go marching
Through the Mall!

"No longer will I get upset,
Or angry with the alphabet!"

"I did
indeed!"

After that, through fog or drizzle,
Zack was never known to grizzle—
(Which, in London, means to grumble
Loud as any thunder-rumble.)

And A to Z is *still* the rule
Of this particular London school.
Albert Ames goes first each day,
Because his name begins with A.

Albert Ames goes first each night
To brush his teeth,
And light the light.

And who goes last?
Why, Zachary...See?
Because his name begins with Z.

With his position, quite content,
He makes each day a great event.
"Good things come last,"
Declares Miss Midge,
When walking over London Bridge.

And all the boys clap long and hard
For Zachary Zween, their strong rear guard.